For Ali Bateman   H.M.

For Deborah and David   N.J.

With thanks to farmer Richard Aldous
for his technical assistance

First published 1986 by
Walker Books Ltd
184-192 Drummond Street
London NW1 3HP

First printed 1986
Printed and bound by L.E.G.O., Vicenza, Italy

British Library Cataloguing in Publication Data
Maisner, Heather
Sam for sale. — (The Tractors of Thomson's Yard)
I. Title II. Johnson, Norman III. Series
823'.914[J] PZ7

ISBN 0-7445-0418-X

SAM
FOR SALE

WRITTEN BY

HEATHER MAISNER

ILLUSTRATED BY

NORMAN JOHNSON

WALKER BOOKS
LONDON

It was almost the end of harvest. Tractor Sam, too old to work, dozed in the yard. Rufus the cart-horse swished flies away with his tail.

A black saloon car swerved and stopped at the gate to Thomson's Yard. The driver and his son leant on the gate, staring at Sam, who was singing his song:

> 'I'm a tractor, my name is Sam,
> I've known Farmer T. since he sat in his pram.
> Despite my rust, I'm the sort you can trust,
> I'm still a fine tractor, oh yes I am.'

A black saloon car stopped at the gate.

They strolled up the drive and knocked at the farmhouse door. When Farmer Thomson and Rosemary came out, the man asked to buy Sam.

'He wouldn't be much use, sir,' laughed Farmer Thomson. 'He's all rust now. Been here for years.'

'That doesn't matter,' said the man. 'We want him for our new tractor museum. He may be the only tractor of his kind in the country.'

'But Sam's not for sale,' said Rosemary quickly.

'He'd have a good home,' the man smiled. 'And we'd give you a good price.'

At that Farmer Thomson agreed. He shook hands with the man and the boy. They said they would come back the next day.

'He's all rust now. Been here for years.'

That night the wind began to blow and there was a hint of rain in the air. The tractors couldn't sleep, and all the animals crept up close to Sam. Nobody wanted him to go. Sam's rusty parts creaked as he fidgeted.

'I'm too old for change,' he sighed. 'I want to stay here with my friends.'

Suddenly Kate, the red tractor, had an idea.

'Let's go on strike,' she said. 'Let's turn on our lights and run down our batteries so we won't start.'

'We can't strike,' said tractor Jack. 'We've the harvest to finish.'

In a pretty pattern across the fields the bales lay waiting to be carted. If the rains came, the straw would be ruined.

All the animals crept up close to Sam.

'I know,' said Rufus, the cart-horse. 'If you two tractors go on strike, Farmer Thomson will have to use Sam to get the bales in. Then he won't sell him.'

The animals and tractors cheered up at once, but Sam was worried.

'I haven't worked for ages,' he mumbled. 'I hope my engine will start.'

'Of course it will,' said Kate with conviction. 'Goody, a day off at last.' She giggled and switched on her lights. Jack switched on his too. For the rest of the night the yard was lit up like a theatre until the batteries died and the lights went out.

The yard was lit up like a theatre.

Next day the sky was a dark cloudy blue.

'Hurry up, Rosemary!' called Farmer Thomson. 'There's a storm on the way.'

He climbed into tractor Jack and turned the starter. Nothing happened. He tried again. Nothing happened.

'Goodness gracious, a flat battery,' he said.

He climbed into Kate and turned the starter. Nothing happened. He tried again. Nothing happened.

'I don't believe it. Another flat battery,' he said.

His face was as dark and angry as the sky.

Along the main road, his loader high with bales, came the neighbour's tractor, Len. He looked at Jack and Kate, and laughed to see they weren't working.

'You tractors are useless!' he shouted. 'You can't even get the bales in on time. If I were Farmer Thomson, I wouldn't just sell Sam, I'd sell the lot of you.'

'You tractors are useless!' Len shouted.

Farmer Thomson watched Len go.

'That's it. I'll hire Len to bring in the bales,' he said.

'No,' said Rosemary. 'Why not use Sam?'

'That useless heap of rust won't even start,' said Farmer Thomson.

But Rosemary was sure he would. She bent down, pulled out Sam's choke and put in the starting handle. She turned it once, she turned it twice. Not a sound.

Sam closed his eyes and tightened his lips. Rosemary turned the handle once and she turned it twice. Sam's engine spluttered and coughed, then stopped.

Once more Sam closed his eyes. Rosemary turned the handle once. Sam spluttered. She turned it twice. Sam coughed. She turned it three times. He spluttered and coughed and rumbled till he roared.

⇌ *Sam's engine spluttered and coughed.* ⇌

Creaking and cranking, Sam started down the drive with the loader.

'Hurrah!' cried Jack. 'Hurrah!' cried Kate.

'Well I never . . . Who would have thought?' Farmer Thomson scratched his ear. Then Sam started to sing:

'I'm a tractor, my name is Sam,
I've known Farmer T. since he sat in his pram.
Despite my rust, I'm the sort you can trust,
I'm still a fine tractor, oh yes I am.'

From the shed to the field and the field to the shed, Sam moved with bales held high. The wind blew strong and the rain splattered down, but still he brought back the bales. When the storm finally broke, all the bales were under cover.

Sam moved with bales held high.

Later the black saloon car pulled up at the farm. The boy opened the gate and the man strode up the drive, holding open his cheque-book and reaching for his pen. Farmer Thomson came out of the house and stepped firmly in front of Sam.

'I'm sorry,' he said, 'Sam's not for sale.'

'But we need him for our museum,' said the man.

'And I need him for my farm,' Farmer Thomson replied. 'Sam saved the bales today. He's not for sale.'

Next day Jack and Kate set off early for the fields. Sam stood waiting for work. But as the sun warmed his body, first one eye, then the other, slowly closed. Soon he dozed peacefully in the yard, repeating over and over the last line of his song:

'I'm still a fine tractor, oh yes I am.'

⇜ *'Sam's not for sale.'* ⇝